Rhythm and Blues

A Story About Doing Right When You Feel Wronged

Featuring the Psalty family of characters
created by Ernie and Debby Rettino

Written by Ken Gire
Illustrated by John Dickenson,
Matt Mew, and Bob Payne

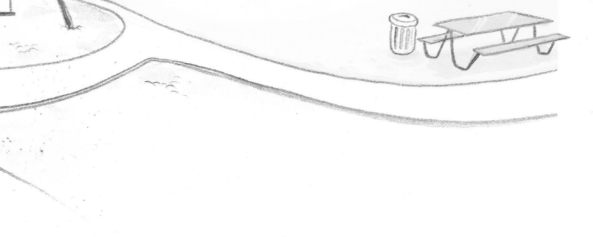

From Focus on the Family Publishing/Maranatha! for Kids
Pomona, CA 91799. Distributed by Word Books, Waco, Texas.

© Copyright 1988 Focus on the Family Publishing

Psalty family of characters are copyright Ernie Rettino and Debby Rettino, and are administered worldwide by Maranatha! Music as follows: Psalty © 1980; Psaltina © 1982; Melody, Harmony, Rhythm © 1982; Charity Churchmouse © 1984; Provolone, Mozzarella and Limburger (Cheeses for Jesus) © 1984; Churchmouse Choir © 1984; Risky Rat © 1984. These characters are trademarks and service marks of Ernie Rettino and Debby Rettino. Maranatha! for Kids and Kids' Praise are trademarks of Maranatha! Music.

No part of this book may be reproduced or copied without written permission from the publisher.

Library of Congress Catalog Card Number 87-81591
ISBN 084-9999-952

"Whe-e-e!" Rhythm screeched, shooting down the playground slide.

"Wo-o-ow!" he hollared, as he flew through the air on a swing.

"Whoa!" he screamed, teetering on the teeter-totter with his friend, a full-of-fun coloring book.

He played with an alphabet book, too. But the book talked real strange.

"S is for swing, a super-swell thing," the book said as he swang. "T is for tree, terrific to see," he recited as he walked by a tree.

The book was so busy practicing his alphabet that he never gave Rhythm a chance to say anything.

So Rhythm skipped over to the monkey bars to play. He was followed by three brightly-colored comic books.

''Hey, you,'' one of them said, pointing at Rhythm.

''Who? Me?'' Rhythm asked, trying to be polite as he hung from the monkey bars.

''I've got a riddle for you,'' the comic book said, winking at his two friends. ''What's funnier looking than a monkey hanging on monkey bars?''

Rhythm replied, "I don't know."

"*You*, monkey face!"

All the comic books burst out laughing and started chanting, "Monkey face from outer space, don't you know you're out of place?"

That hurt Rhythm's feelings. He hung his head as he got down from the bars and went to another part of the park.

He saw a couple of encyclopedias playing on the merry-go-round and hoped they would ask him to play with them.

''You can jump on if you can tell us how many feet make a mile complete,'' called out one of the know-it-all encyclopedias.

Rhythm knew a mile was very, very long, but he had no idea exactly how long. Feeling embarrassed, he walked away with his shoulders slumped.

Then he came back to the teeter-totters, where an overweight dictionary sat.

"Greetings and salutations," called the dictionary. "Please join me in this immeasurably pleasurable pastime."

Rhythm had never heard anyone talk like that before! He thought for a while and realized the dictionary wanted him to get on the teeter-totter. "No thanks," replied Rhythm.

An unkind look suddenly clouded the dictionary's face. "Feeling frightened, you diminutive, spine-headed booklet, you?" he smirked.

That made Rhythm mad, especially because he wasn't sure what all of the big words meant. "I'm not scared," he said.

So he got on the teeter-totter to show this big bully he wasn't afraid.

The dictionary weighed so much that Rhythm's end of the teeter-totter shot straight up. Now how was he going to get down?

The dictionary roared with laughter. "It seems you are suffering a twinge of trepidation."

Rhythm hardly understood anything the dictionary said. And he was getting really scared. So he begged, "Please let me down!"

"As per my usual utterance," the dictionary responded, "your wish is my command." Suddenly the dictionary hopped off the teeter-totter, sending Rhythm crashing to the ground!

Landing with a THUD, he was so surprised that he started to cry.

"Blubbering booklets make me ill," the dictionary announced, with his nose stuck up in the air.

When Rhythm heard these unkind words, he stopped feeling hurt and started feeling angry.

Clenching his teeth and fists, he lunged at the dictionary, who had turned to walk away. He pushed the dictionary down--THUMP. Then Rhythm tore out one of the book's pages--RI-I-I-P.

Before the big book could get up, Rhythm ran off with the page in his hand. He laughed and felt happy that he had got back at the dictionary.

"The big bully," Rhythm said to himself. "I guess I showed him!"

When he got home, Rhythm walked quickly past his father, Psalty the singing songbook, and his mother Psaltina. He went straight to his room and sat on his bed. He looked at the torn page.

"He'll never be able to use these words again," said Rhythm. Then he saw the word "enemy" on the page and read the definition: "A person who hates another and who tries to injure him."

"From now on, I'm not going to let my enemies bully me. I'm going to get even!"

When Rhythm looked up, he was surprised to see Psalty standing in the doorway, carrying a ball and mitt.

"Rhythm, how about playing catch?"

Quickly the booklet tried to hide the torn page under his pillow.

"Uh, uh, hi, Dad."

"Hi, Rhythm. What have you got there?"

"Oh, nothing important."

"May I see it?" asked Psalty.

Rhythm slowly took the dictionary's page from beneath the pillow and gave it to his dad. He could feel his face growing hot as he did.

"Where did you get this?" questioned Psalty.

"On the playground," replied Rhythm.

"Just lying on the ground?"

"Well, it was lying on the ground . . . in a dictionary," Rhythm explained.

"How did you get it then?"

"Well . . . I sort of . . . took it," Rhythm confessed.

"You mean you tore it out of the dictionary?" asked his dad.

Rhythm nodded.

"Oh, Rhythm," Psalty said, "that makes me so sad."

"But, Dad, you don't understand...he was a bully...he picked on me," Rhythm defended himself.

"And so you got even."

"I just did to him what he did to me."

"That's not how Jesus tells us to live, is it, Rhythm?" Psalty asked.

The little booklet became silent.

"Jesus wants us to treat others like we want to be treated. He told us to love our enemies—not to hate them. Instead of getting even, Jesus wants us to pray for those who hurt us."

"But how do you love somebody that's so . . . so . . . so unlovable?" Rhythm asked, feeling confused.

Psalty pointed to a picture on the wall that showed Jesus on the cross. "Do you remember what Jesus prayed when all of those mean people made fun of Him and hurt Him?"

Rhythm slowly looked up at the picture. He nodded. "Yes. He said, 'Father, forgive these people, for they don't know what they are doing.'"

Rhythm's eyes lit up with understanding.

"And that's how we can love the unlovable," Psalty said, "by forgiving them, not by getting even."

"Can we pray, Dad?" Rhythm asked.

"Sure, Rhythm."

"Lord, please help me to love those who are hard to love. Thank You that You will help me," Rhythm prayed.

Then Psalty and Rhythm went to find the dictionary so Rhythm could give back the torn page.

When they came to the park, they saw the dictionary
sitting at one of the picnic tables, with his head in his hands.

Rhythm took a deep breath and walked up to the big bully. He was afraid, but he knew he was doing the right thing.

"I'm s-s-sorry for hurting you and tearing out your page," Rhythm said, getting ready to run as he handed the page back to the dictionary. "Please f-f-forgive me. I was mad, and I was just trying to get even by hurting you. But that was wrong."

To Rhythm's surprise, the dictionary didn't hit him or even act mad. The big book just sat there looking hurt.

Finally the dictionary said, ''I'm sorry, too. I acted like a big bully and used words I knew you didn't understand because you're not a dictionary. Will you forgive me?''

''Yes,'' Rhythm answered.

''I forgive you, too,'' the dictionary offered.

Then Rhythm gently placed the page back in the dictionary.

"Do you want to play with me?" the dictionary asked.

"Sure!" Rhythm answered. "I'd like that!"

So they slipped down the slide and screamed, "Whe-e-e!" They swung on the swings and hollared, "Wo-o-ow!" They even teetered on the totter and screeched, "Whoa!"

While they were playing, Rhythm thought about how much better it felt to forgive than to get even. He smiled at the dictionary, and the dictionary smiled back. Rhythm knew he had found a new friend.